WAFFLES CAN'T DANCE

Written by **Qwen Lewis**

Illustrated by **Katerina Golivets**

Blueberry is having a party and Waffle thinks he doesn't stand a chance. Everyone knows that waffles can't dance.

Bacon is the best breakdancer you would ever meet. The Egg Twins scramble on the dance floor perfectly to the beat.

Waffle visits all of his friends asking each one for advice.

They all reply,

"Just have fun feel the beat and don't think twice."

Waffle's first visit was to his friend Butter.

Waffle attempts to glide like Butter.

What happens next will make you shutter.
Waffle's slide turns into a roll.
He's upside down no longer on his toes.

"Pop your body to the beat, then tic toc like a clock", Bacon teaches Waffle while dancing like a robot.

Waffle moves his arms
to tic and to toc but instead
Waffle's body goes flop!

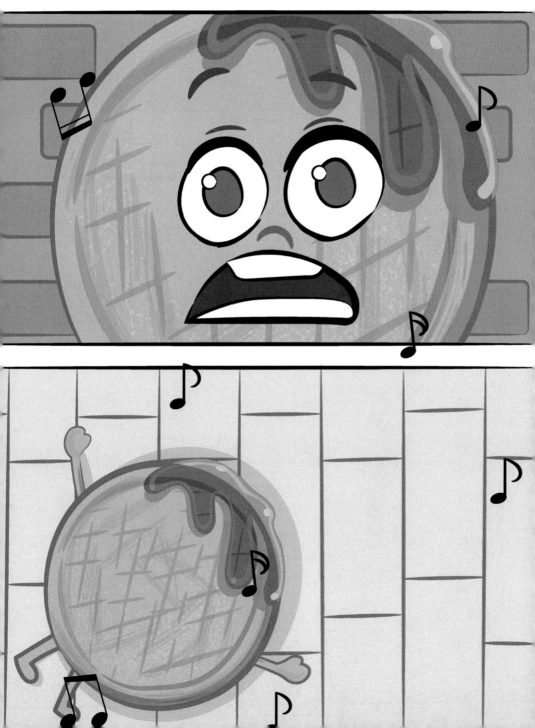

Waffle heads to the party remembering his friends' encouraging words.

He says aloud,
"I will be brave!
I will have fun!
I will dance like a bird!"

Waffle makes his way to the dance floor and moves his arms to the beat.
His legs feel the rhythm and it slides the vibe to his feet.

Waffle's feet are jamming!

Waffle's fluffy center starts to jiggle. He's having so much fun he doesn't notice the extra wiggle.

Left foot, right foot.
One, two, three, four.

SPLAT!!!

It's too late.
Waffle is face down on the
dance mat.

"I have to get up",
- Waffle whispers
to himself.

Waffle tells Butter as he offers to help.

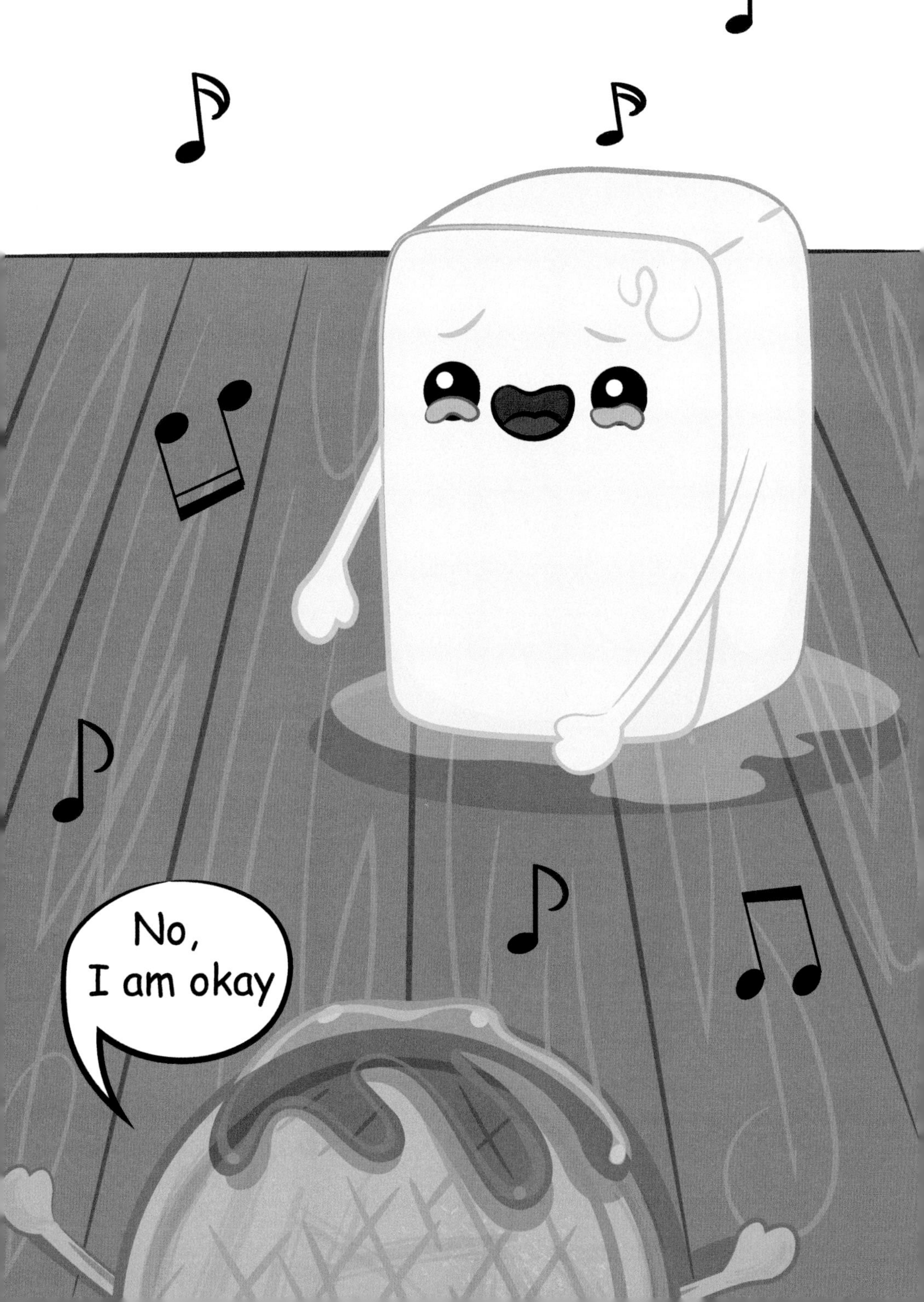

Waffle gives himself a wiggle,
then a waggle;
like a fish onshore.

He looks up to see his friends still
dancing on the dance floor.

DJ Orange changes the tune and Waffle's excitement can't hide.

"This is my favorite song! Waffle says as his body catches the vibe."

Back and forth Waffle moves his body still flat on the floor.

DJ Orange catches a glimpse and yells.

One by one Waffle's friends crowd around him praising his cool dance moves. Waffle continues to roll to the rhythm then back onto his shoes.

Who knew Waffle had it in him all along!
He let go of his fear and allowed his body to take over the song.

Now Waffle is always on the dance floor showing off his dance moves.

Having a good time, being himself with nothing to prove.

This book is dedicated to:
<u>YOU</u> little reader!
In a world of trends and likes
never forget that
the coolest thing
you could ever be
is yourself.

Qwen Lewis♡